Max and Molly
The Raven Thief

Written by Sally Doherty

Illustrated by Sonny Fletcher

Collins

Chapter 1

We made it.

My first trip out of town in six months. Not far – only a 40-minute drive. But that's more than enough of a battering for my body. Being in a car used to rock me gently to sleep. Now, it's like being rattled around in a tin can with an electric drill inside my head.

Mum opens the door, and the sea air rushes in. Dad loads our stuff out of the boot: picnic rug, towels, deckchairs – and my wheelchair. He brings it round to my side, and I haul myself into it.

Monty springs out of the car, shaking his red fur from his head to the tip of his tail. Dad grabs the end of his lead, and I hold it too. Then we're off, Dad wheeling me along the quay with Monty trotting in front, like he's my horse and I'm in a chariot. Or, better yet, he's a dragon pulling my superjet. A group of passers-by stare, and I scowl. Anything different, and people have to stare.

Plunder Cove

Mum and Lily follow, their arms full. The wind catches Lily's long, blonde hair and smacks her in the face. I stifle a giggle. She shoots me a sideways glare. If Lily had superpowers, she would fry me in an instant. Good job she doesn't. Mum says she's going through a teenager phase, and I should ignore her. *Sisters.* Who'd have them?

"Hold up." Mum brings us all to a halt. "I need to get some water at the shop."

A newspaper stand leans against the wall. "*Notorious Burglar Strikes Again*". On the newspapers is a blurry image of a man who could be anyone.

Dad picks up a copy. "Please can you get this for me too?"

Mum points to a notice. "Cash only. Anyone got any money? This village is stuck in time!"

Dad fumbles in his pocket and hands her some coins.

She heads into a little building with a thatched roof and whitewashed walls. There's a sign over the door – *A Scoop a Day* – and a picture of a dripping ice-cream cone.

A crowd strolls out, laughing and shouting. I cover my ears. Noise is so much louder since I fell ill with M.E.

Dad wheels me into a quiet corner, while Monty strains at his lead, desperate to be part of everything. Sometimes, I wish he wasn't quite so friendly. I shake his bag of dog biscuits, and he focuses all his attention on me.

"Sit!" I say.

He plops his bottom down so quickly, he almost topples over. Anything for food. He takes the biscuit and munches happily.

I lean back, breathing in the salty air, and get a whiff of rotten food. *Bleugh!* I'm near a little alleyway between the shop and the quay wall. A bin overflowing with empty chip cartons blocks the entrance. Behind it, I hear muffled voices.

"It has to be today." That's a woman's voice. "It gets picked up at 3 o'clock this afternoon."

I peer into the alley. Two shadowy figures hover inside.

"And there's enough is there?" replies a man.

"Woof! Woof woof!" Monty leaps at a passing seagull.

The voices fall silent, and the figures drop back into the alley.

Chapter 2

"Max!" A girl comes out of the ice-cream shop.

I wince. I recognise her from school, but I don't know her. When you only manage half days at school (and sometimes none at all), then you don't make many friends.

I worry about seeing people who know me. Worry that they'll wonder why I can go on a trip out but not go to school every day. But it doesn't work like that. Some days, I feel well enough to do things and some days I don't.

The girl doesn't comment though. She's too busy stroking Monty whose tail is rotating faster than a helicopter propeller.

"Mayling!" A man pops his head round the door. "We're busy in here! You're supposed to be finding Sarah."

"Sorry, Baba!" Mayling turns to me. "My parents own the ice-cream shop. I help in the summer holidays."

Now *that* is cool. "Do you get to eat as much ice cream as you want?" I ask.

She laughs. "I'm allowed one a day. It gets a bit much after a while though."

"You can never have too much ice cream!"

She grins at me, and I find myself smiling back.

"Mayling!" yells her dad again.

"OK, OK!" Mayling scours the crowd. "Seen a woman wearing a beige apron? She's supposed to be working."

"I don't think so," I say.

Mayling cups her mouth and shouts, "Sarah!"

A woman emerges from the alleyway. "Just having a break."

9

"Down there?!" says Mayling.

The woman stalks into the shop.

Mayling gives me a wave. "Catch you later!" Her dark hair swings as she jogs back into *A Scoop a Day.*

I peer behind the smelly bin. I'm sure there had been two people, not just one.

A massive bird swoops out of the alley with a loud "caw", and I almost fall out of my wheelchair. It perches on the roof of the shop and flaps its black, ragged wings.

A man squeezes round the bin. He pulls
his grey baseball cap low over dark sunglasses
and scurries off.

I knew there had been two people!

I'm watching him when Mum appears, clutching
water bottles.

Dad takes the handles of the wheelchair. "Ready?"
he says.

The man has disappeared. I dart a glance at the bird;
its beady eyes pierce into me.

A breeze rustles round the quayside, and I shiver.
The sooner we get out of here, the better. I flick
Monty's lead. "To the beach!"

We head for the slipway and immediately hit
a problem – a high kerb with no lowered section. It's like
the world doesn't care about people like me. Dad turns
the wheelchair and has to jerk it up backwards. My whole
body jolts.

Now for the slipway. And boy, is it steep.
Like REALLY steep. I clench my teeth. If Dad accidentally
lets go, I'll career straight into the sea. Either that or
faceplant into a rock.

And then at the bottom, we hit problem number three.
It turns out wheelchairs don't work on sand. We should
have realised that.

What on earth are we going to do?

Chapter 3

"Guess I'll have to carry you," says Dad.

No way.

I weigh up my options:

1) Try and walk.
2) Stay in the car while the rest of my family is having fun on the beach.
3) Let Dad carry me like I'm two instead of eleven.

People are building up behind us, and we're causing chaos. Meanwhile, Monty is getting all three of his legs tangled in his lead and almost trips himself up – as well as a passing granny.

I wobble to my feet. Maybe I can do this. I take a few steps, and the sand sucks at my energy like I'm walking through treacle. I don't need the wheelchair at home, but walking after a drive? *Not a chance.*

Dad runs his fingers through his brown, curly hair and braces himself. "Climb aboard, matey!"

I roll my eyes. Could he *be* more embarrassing?

He lifts me and balances me over his shoulder. He's tall and gangly, and suddenly I'm miles off the ground. My head swims.

We set off across the sand. Lily stomps along behind, trying to control Monty as well as carrying deckchairs and towels. Meanwhile, I'm bumping around on Dad's back with my bottom sticking up for everyone to see. *Excellent.*

Dad stops halfway across the beach. "This should do."

I slither off and plop onto the picnic rug. Dad's puffing and panting, and I'm taking deep breaths, trying to recover. You'd think I was the one who'd had to carry several kilos of body weight.

Monty nuzzles my hand, then licks all the way up my arm. It would be cute if I hadn't just seen that same tongue licking a clump of rotting seaweed.

I take in the scene. Waves foam at the shore, and seagulls whirl overhead. I'm actually out. Not at home. Not at school. But out.

"Keep your eyes peeled." Dad winks. "Smugglers used to hide stolen goods in this cove."

I shudder as the sun disappears behind a cloud.

Dad grabs the tennis ball. "Anyone for a game of catch?"

Monty is leaping at the ball before the words have fully left Dad's mouth. Most of the time I forget Monty's missing a leg; he's so speedy and bouncy. I think he forgets too. He takes corners too fast in the garden, and next thing you know, he's skidding along on his stump.

"Want to join in, Max?" asks Dad.

I find the tennis ball launcher which makes it easier for me to throw, and manoeuvre myself into a deckchair. "Ready."

Monty lets out a volley of excited barks.

Dad passes me the ball, and I fire it into the air.

Monty is off quicker than I can say, "Goooo". His paws pound on the sand, his mouth open and his ears flapping.

The ball soars upwards and plummets down in an arc. Down, down, down.

Monty's staring at the ball so intently that he doesn't notice where he's heading. He jumps up, catches it in his mouth and lands right on top of a man sitting nearby. A man wearing a grey baseball cap and dark sunglasses. The man I saw earlier lurking in the alleyway.

Chapter 4

The man's cup of tea flies everywhere, spraying him from head to toe in hot liquid. He gives a roar of anger.

There's the beating of wings above, and the massive bird appears, circling overhead.

Tea drips from the man's chin, and Monty licks it.

Dad runs over. "Sorry! Sorry!"

"Get him away from me!"

Dad drags Monty away.

The man searches his pockets for a tissue. Then tears a handful of pages from a notepad instead and wipes himself down. Shooting us a glare, he puts up a beach umbrella and disappears from view.

With a final clap of its wings, the bird settles on the edge of the cliff.

"Sorry," I whisper to Dad.

We catch each other's eye, and I see that he's trying not to laugh. A grin forms on my lips.

"Behave, you two!" says Mum.

Dad straightens his face. "Maybe this isn't the best game right now."

Mum scours the shore. "I think I might dip my toe in the sea … if you don't mind, Max?"

"No, it's fine." I try to ignore the ripple of jealousy trickling through me.

"Coming, Lily?" says Mum.

My sister is staring at her phone. "There's no reception!"

"Well, you are on the beach. Maybe you can manage without your mobile for a few hours?"

Lily scowls, pulls on her headphones and lies down.

"I'll come," says Dad. "Shall we take Monty?"

"Yep." Monty is mine. We got him a year ago, after I fell ill. Mum and Dad walk him, and the rest of the time, he's my cuddle buddy.

I pull my sketchbook out of my bag and lean back in the deckchair for support. Drawing lets me escape. My body never stops grumbling. But when I'm drawing, I can forget it a bit. I flip through the pages and find a blank one. Studying the view, I trace the outline of the rocks.

I'm chewing my tongue in concentration, when something tickles my leg. A scrap of paper. Not mine. This one's got lines, and the edge is ripped like it's been torn out of a notepad. I look around – did it come from the grey-cap man?

I squint at the paper: a list of the days of the week with a number next to each of them. £1,781. £1,225. £1,364 … At the end, next to Saturday, there's a total circled in bold red pen. There's a date next to it too. 2nd August.

Today is Saturday. Today is 2nd August. And that is a LOT of money. What does it mean?

Sunday £1,781
Monday £1,225
Tuesday £1,364
Wednesday £1,448
Thursday £1,389
Friday £1,667
Saturday £1,823

2nd August £10,697

Chapter 5

Mum, Dad and Monty stroll back up the beach. Monty is soaking, and sand sticks to his wet fur. He looks like a bedraggled rat. Well, a giant bedraggled rat. He shakes and showers me with water.

"Sorry!" says Mum. "We couldn't keep him out of the sea. You know what he's like."

I wonder if I should mention the piece of paper to her, but the man is still hiding behind the umbrella, and he seemed pretty angry last time we bothered him.

"Who's for an ice cream?" says Dad.

"Me!" I say. I want to shout, but that's a bit beyond me.

Lily removes her headphones and looks mildly interested for once. "I'll come."

"I'll stay with Max," says Mum.

I *hate* that this illness stops other people doing things too. "It's OK, you can go. I need to rest."

Mum frowns. "You sure? I don't like leaving you by yourself."

I need some quiet. "As long as you bring me a chocolate ice cream with extra chocolate on top."

She smiles. "On it."

I watch them set off and lower myself onto the picnic rug. Dad has left the newspaper out, and the headline catches my eye once more: *"Notorious Burglar Strikes Again."*

I read on:

Notorious Burglar Strikes Again

Following a spate of burglaries at shops around the country, police are hunting for a man in his forties, armed with a highly vicious creature. Do not approach.

With a shudder, I turn the paper over so I can't see it.

I lie back and put on my headphones. These ones aren't blaring music like Lily's, just shutting out noise so my brain can calm down. I place an eye mask over my eyes. Daylight is bright even if it's not sunny.

Monty settles with his head on my leg. I love it when he does this. My limbs loosen, and my muscles relax. Rest is boring but necessary. It means I can do stuff at other times. Well, not big stuff. But little stuff.

As my breathing slows, I hear voices nearby. Two of them. And they sound like the people who were whispering in the alleyway.

"Everything ready?" says the male voice.

I can just make it out over my headphones.

"The money is all bagged up." That's the female voice.

My muscles stiffen.

"Keep your voice down!" says the man.

A waft of strong sweat seeps up my nostrils, and I try not to gag.

"He can't hear. He's listening to music," she replies.

Are they talking about me? I'm not actually listening to music. *Ha ha to them.*

I hold my breath and strain to hear. *Max the Super Spy on a mission.*

Chapter 6

"I'll strike in ten minutes." The man's voice is low and gruff.

The woman hesitates. "I'm not sure we should do this. The family needs the money – the mum's not well."

"It's no good getting attached to the people each time, sis! We need the money too, don't we? I could still have my own ice-cream shop. But no. They had to close me down."

"A customer found mouse droppings in the mint choc chip! They ate it! They thought it was the choc chip."

I almost burst out laughing despite the nerves trickling through me.

"Engelbert was supposed to eat that mouse! Not let it run riot in the shop. How else am I supposed to make money now?" he spits. "No one will hire me."

Slowly, I raise my arm and knock my eye mask off. It *is* the two people who were in the alleyway. Sarah and grey-cap man. But who's Engelbert?

The wind ripples the pages in the newspaper. *Burglar Strikes Again ... armed with a highly vicious creature ...*

The realisation hits me like a jolt of lightning, and my stomach does a full somersault. The burglars are here, and I'm lying right next to them.

On the cliff, the bird lets out a sharp caw. It opens its wings and nosedives into the sand, emerging with a shiny coin in its sharp beak.

"Ha! He's at it already." The man raises an arm, and the bird swoops over. It lands on his sleeve and drops the coin into his palm. "I've trained you well, haven't I? Best raven around." The man ruffles its neck feathers, and the bird flexes its long talons.

"What's the code word this time?" asks Sarah. "If I need to stop Engelbert attacking someone?"

"You won't. He'll just scare them so he can seize the money. But he'll abort the mission if you say 'plump mouse'."

"Plump mouse," she repeats. "I best get back so they don't get suspicious."

"If Engelbert does his job, the family won't even know you're involved," says her brother. "I'll see you in ten minutes."

"This is the last time I'm helping you!"

30

She walks past, and I clamp my eyes shut. I hear the man clearing up his belongings and setting off after her.

Once he's gone, I sit bolt upright.

Five minutes ago, I was in desperate need of a rest. Now, adrenaline is pounding inside me. While it's usually not wise to push past my energy limits, sometimes there's no choice. I'll crash later, but I have to deal with this. My whole family is in the ice-cream shop, and they're about to be attacked by a highly vicious raven.

I need to warn them, but how? I'm trapped on this rug in a desert of sand.

Monty pushes his head into my hand, and I stroke his ears. He gives a little whine. *Wait* – Monty! Maybe he can get help.

A family is sitting at the other end of the beach. Too far for me to shout, but maybe Monty could get their attention.

I pick up the tennis ball and the launcher.

Monty's ears prick up.

"Ready, boy? Remember what you did earlier? When you disturbed that man? I need you to do the same again."

Chapter 7

I aim the tennis ball at the family and send it flying.
It soars upwards, and Monty sprints after it.

Right on target, it lands in the middle of the family.
Bull's-eye!

Monty takes a giant leap … and splats down on
the toddler's ice cream.

The toddler screams. The mum screams and yanks
Monty away.

Meanwhile, I'm summoning all my energy to flap
my arms. "Over here! I need your help!"

The mum shakes her fist and turns away to deal with
the wailing toddler.

Monty bounds back across the beach, ball in his mouth, tongue lolling. He looks so pleased that I don't have the heart to tell him off.

Mission failed.

Burglar-man is hovering at the bottom of the slipway checking his watch. Five minutes to go.

How on earth can I alert my family?

Dad comes out of the ice-cream shop – I can see his head bobbing along above the quay wall.

Look. Look at me. I try to send telepathic thoughts, but Dad is busy devouring his ice cream.

I need to get a message to him. I glance from my sketchbook to Monty, who's slobbering on the ball, and an idea pings into my brain.

Tearing a page out of the book, I scribble what must be the most ridiculous statement in the history of the universe.

The code word
to stop the raven
is plump mouse.

I fold up the note and wrap it around Monty's collar. "You have to take this to Dad, OK?" I wave in the direction of the quay.

Monty stares at me in confusion. Sometimes, I reckon there's nothing going on in that head of his at all.

"Dad! Over there!" I gesticulate wildly.

Monty tilts his head to one side as if to say, "*What are you woofing on about, human?*"

I can't use the tennis ball launcher, it's too far. *Think, think.*

"Biscuit?"

Monty sits to attention.

"Dad! Biscuit!" I point again.

Monty's off, careering across the beach, weaving
through families and buckets and dried seaweed.
He heads for the slipway and passes burglar-man.
The note is still in Monty's collar. He's going to make it.

Then he sniffs the air, veers to the right and pounces
on a stick.

Oh no. If there's one thing Monty loves even more than
biscuits, it's sticks.

He shakes it, tosses it into the air and catches it.
With a happy woof, he gambols back to me, clutching his
new treasure.

Mission Two failed.

Movement at the bottom of the slipway catches
my attention. Burglar-man is on the move. I'm running out
of time.

Chapter 8

A big wave rushes in and almost reaches the picnic blanket. The tide is coming in. The wave retreats, leaving a patch of wet sand. I glance at the stick that Monty's chomping on.

"Sorry, boy, I'm going to need that." I prise it from his jaws, getting slobber all over my fingers. *Yuck.*

Mission Attempt Three, here we come.

I wobble to my feet. I only need to walk a few steps; I can do this.

Heat rises in my face. Is anyone watching who saw me in my wheelchair earlier? People don't understand that some wheelchair-users don't need them all the time. They see us walk, and they think we're faking being unwell or disabled.

Mum tells me to think of it like a car. People use cars to travel long distances, and I use a wheelchair to travel a distance that's long for me. I stand up a bit straighter. It's no one else's business if I can walk or if I need a wheelchair.

"Max!" says a voice behind me.

"Mayling!"

She smiles. "My baba said I could come and join you for a bit."

"Your shop! It's about to be burgled!"

Her jaw drops. "What?"

"The woman who works for you – Sarah – her brother is going to steal all the money! I heard them talking about it."

"We need that money! My mama … she's not well. We're saving for a stairlift." Mayling turns to run. "I have to get back!"

Behind her, burglar-man is striding up the slipway, the raven on his shoulder.

"You'll be too late!" I reach out a hand. "We need to get a message to my dad." I take another step.

In big letters, I write in the wet sand with Monty's stick:

Mayling frowns in bewilderment. "Plump mouse?"

"No time to explain! We need to get my dad's attention." I try to wave and shout, but I'm all out of energy.

"What's your dad's name?" she asks.

"Steve."

"Steve! STEVE!" yells Mayling, flapping her arms like she's about to take off.

Dad's attention is still focused entirely on munching his ice cream.

"Monty! Bark!" I command.

Monty stares at me.

"Seriously? Most of the time, I can't get you to stop barking, but *now* you want to be silent?"

We can see the top half of burglar-man walking along the quay.

Mayling yells, "STEVE!", at the top of her lungs.

Finally, Dad looks down at the beach.

I point at my message. I can see the confusion on his face even from here.

"Attack!" shouts the burglar.

The raven opens its enormous wings and flies into the ice-cream shop. A piercing scream comes from inside. My heart shoots into my mouth. Was that Mum?

Dad's head snaps away from us.

Chapter 9

I grab the stick. I'll have to do a sketch. I draw well on paper, don't I? So why should this be any different? Quickly, I outline the raven in the sand.

Dad is frozen, glued to the quay wall.

Look back at us. Look back at us, I urge.

Shrieks and caws sound from the shop.

"Montgomery Archibald Rufus! BARK!" I shout.

Monty opens his mouth and barks as loud as thunder.

My dad peers at us again.

I point between my drawing and the message. Mayling joins in, pointing at the message and then the shop.

Dad hesitates, and time seems to slow down. And then he cries, "Plump mouse!"

The raven flaps out of the door in a cloud of black feathers.

"No!" screams the burglar. "Attack!"

The raven spins in the air about to re-enter the shop.

"Plump mouse!" yells Dad and launches himself at the burglar before he can send the raven back inside. They tumble to the ground out of sight.

With an ear-splitting screech, the bird zooms into the sky and disappears from view.

"Your dad did it! He did it!" Mayling beams at me.

I point at the quay. "I wouldn't be so sure."

Sarah is racing out of the ice-cream shop, a sack clutched in her arms.

Mayling sets off running, her hair flying behind her. She tears up the slipway and charges for the woman. But she's not quick enough. Sarah dodges her and jogs down onto the sand.

I try to lift my legs, but they're like lead. All I can do is watch as she flies past. At the end of the beach, a flight of steps leads to the cliff path. She's heading straight for it. She's going to escape with the money, and there's nothing I can do about it.

45

I'm still holding the stick in my hand, and Monty tries to grab it playfully.

The stick!

Without giving myself time to think, I hurl it across the beach right under Sarah's feet. She trips over and crashes to the floor, a tangle of arms and legs. The sack lands several feet away from me, and coins pour out. I can't quite reach it.

Sarah scrambles to her feet, but Monty leaps into the air and lands on top of her. She sprawls back onto the ground. With a happy woof, he licks her face like it's all one big game.

Puffing and panting, Mayling arrives and grabs the money. "Nice one," she says.

I lie down right where I am. The sand is damp and cold, but I don't even notice. My whole body feels like it's just run a marathon – while dragging an elephant, who's wearing iron boots. But inside my spirit is soaring.

Mission Three successful.

47

Chapter 10

I wheel into *A Scoop a Day*. If it were my shop, I'd call it *Three Scoops a Day*. One is definitely not enough.

Dad pushes me around the wooden tables and chairs – there's space for us to get through, which is better than most shops.

I've been resting on the beach for two whole hours. It took that long for my body to stop screaming at me. It was an hour before I could mutter a few words. Mum hovered nearby like a distressed butterfly. I know she finds it hard not to be able to do anything to help. But the only thing that works is quiet.

I settle into the sofa and lean against the squishy cushions. Outside, a police siren wails in the distance. I missed all the excitement. But apparently, they've been hunting those burglars for over three years! I might get a medal and everything.

Mayling plops down next to me.

Her dad comes out from behind the counter. "Here's the hero of the hour!"

I blush. "It wasn't just me. Mayling helped. And so did Monty, didn't you, boy?" I ruffle his ears.

"When I told you to keep your eyes peeled for stolen goods, I didn't actually mean it!" laughs my own dad.

It's funny how things turn out. If I was well, I'd have been too busy racing around to notice the burglars right under my nose.

A woman appears from the back of the shop and rolls over to us. She's in a wheelchair too. "You really did save us. We'd be lost without that money. Is there anything we can do to repay you?"

My eyes scan the counter bursting with different flavours: chocolate, strawberry, cookie dough, honeycomb … "How about a free ice cream?"

"Free ice cream for life!" says Mayling's dad. "Now what will it be?"

My mouth waters. How will I ever choose?

"How about mint choc chip?" Dad winks.

Everyone groans – by now, they all know the tale of the mouse droppings.

Mayling's dad hands me the biggest ice cream I've ever seen. Half chocolate, half salted caramel. Well, I couldn't be expected to choose only one flavour, could I?

Monty gets a dollop of cream, and he wolfs it down before I've taken the first lick of mine.

Lily lifts her headphones to say, "That was pretty cool, what you did. Well done, bro," before disappearing back into her music.

My jaw drops. Maybe sisters aren't that bad, after all.

As we leave for home, I spot a flash of black feathers on the cliff. The raven? But when I look again, it's gone.

Mayling waves from the shop door. "I'll see you at school!"

I can't help a smile forming on my lips. Did I just make a friend?

"And don't forget, free ice cream for life!" calls her dad.

I grin. Now *that* is something I won't forget.

Monty woofs in agreement and sets off pulling my superjet. Team Pawsome save the day. Ready for our next mission (after a good rest).

Plunder Cove

Nailed it!

Statement from the defence

Mr Biddle has received terrible treatment at the hands of the law. Following one minor mistake, his ice-cream shop was closed without any opportunity for second chances. With his reputation tarnished, he was unable to find work, leaving him and his sister struggling to afford necessities such as food and clothes (Exhibit A). Furthermore, he cannot be held responsible for the burgling behaviour of a raven (Exhibit B).

Exhibit A

Exhibit B

Statement from the prosecution

Over the past three years, Mr Biddle and his sister have stolen tens of thousands of pounds from 20 shops across the nation (Exhibit C). Working with a trained raven, Mr Biddle terrorised shop owners and stole their takings (Exhibit D). Many have been left struggling to make ends meet, and some have been too terrified to return to work. Whatever his own situation, stealing from others is never the answer.

Sunday £1,781
Monday £1,225
Tuesday £1,364
Wednesday £1,448
Thursday £1,389
Friday £1,667
Saturday £1,823

2nd August £10,697

Exhibit C

Exhibit D

Ideas for reading

Written by Christine Whitney
Primary Literacy Consultant

Reading objectives:
- check that the book makes sense to them, discussing their understanding and exploring the meaning of words in context
- draw inferences such as inferring characters' feelings, thoughts and motives
- predict what might happen from details stated and implied
- summarise the main ideas drawn from more than one paragraph
- identify and discuss themes
- provide reasoned justifications for their views

Spoken language objectives:
- participate in discussion
- speculate, hypothesise, imagine and explore ideas through talk
- ask relevant questions

Curriculum links: PSHE education

Interest words: quay, cove, plunder, slipway, tide, shore

Build a context for reading
- Before looking at the book, encourage children to name as many birds as they can in a minute. When finished, ask if anyone knows what a raven is. Show an image of a raven.
- Look at the image on the front cover, then at the title. What does the reader know about the characters in the book prior to reading?
- Ask the group to discuss who they believe is the *feathered fiend*.
- The story is set at the seaside. Ensure understanding of the following words prior to reading – *quay, cove, plunder, slipway, tide, shore*.

Understand and apply reading strategies
- Read Chapter 1 together. Summarise what the reader knows about Max by the end of the chapter.
- Continue to read together up to the end of Chapter 2. Ask children to explain what new information is learned which moves the story plot on.
- Read Chapter 3 together. How does the author make the *man wearing a grey baseball cap* seem suspicious?
- Read Chapter 4. Encourage children to predict what the scrap of paper and the amounts written on it mean.
- In Chapter 5, why is it important that Max's headphones are simply noise cancelling and do not play music? What has Max discovered by the end of this chapter?